MAKING ROOM

JOANNE TAYLOR

Illustrated by

PETER RANKIN

TUNDRA BOOKS

Published in Canada by Tundra Books,
481 University Avenue, Toronto, Ontario M5G 2E9

Published in the United States by Tundra Books of Northern New York,
P.O. Box 1030, Plattsburgh, New York 12901

Library of Congress Control Number: 2004102032

National Library of Canada Cataloguing in Publication

Taylor, Joanne

    Making room / Joanne Taylor ; Peter Rankin, illustrator.

ISBN 0-88776-651-X

    I. Rankin, Peter, 1961- II. Title.

PS8589.A895M33 2004   jC813'.6   C2004-900839-0

We acknowledge the financial support of the Government of Canada through the
Book Publishing Industry Development Program and that of the Government of Ontario
through the Ontario Media Development Corporation's Ontario Book Initiative. We
further acknowledge the support of the Canada Council for the Arts and the Ontario
Arts Council for our publishing program.

Design: KT Njo

Medium: Oil on masonite

Printed and bound in Hong Kong, China

1 2 3 4 5 6   09 08 07 06 05 04

For Jim St.Clair, the keeper of the stories, with great admiration.
J. T.

For my family, especially my wife, Brenda, and my children,
Elizabeth, Angus, Mark, Sarah, and Duncan, my youngest adviser.
P. R.

ACKNOWLEDGMENTS

The illustrator wishes to extend special thanks to
Mary Elizabeth MacInnis, Francis MacNeil, Jim St.Clair, Joanne Taylor,
and the Highland Village Museum, Cape Breton.

John William Smith was barely eighteen when he crossed a shallow river, climbed a steep hill, and looked out over a broad valley. He had one axe and one saw, two calves and two chickens, and strong arms.

"This is where I'll build my home," he said.

And that's what John William did. He chopped trees from the forest and had them milled into boards. Then he built himself a one-room house with a fireplace made of stones he cleared from his own field. He planted three apple trees, a gift from his parents.

"This is all I need," he said each evening as he sat by his door, sipped his tea, and watched the sun set behind the far hills.

After many sunsets alone, John William said, "I think I need . . .

. . . a wife."

He changed his shirt, even though it wasn't Sunday, and went down the hill to the village that was only an hour's walk from his place.

And on a day in early summer, the village gathered at John William's new house for a ceilidh. With the fiddlers playing and the dancers swinging, they celebrated his marriage to Annie MacFarlane, from across the river.

"You're all I need," John William told her that evening as they sat by their door, sipped their tea, and watched the sun set behind the far hills.

Annie made a wonderful wife. She worked hard and she sang as she worked. "John William, dear," Annie said one day, "I think we need . . . a pantry."

"I'll build it right away, my dear," he said.

And that's what John William did. He built a sturdy pantry on the back of the house, with lots of shelves and a good wide counter so Annie could make her bread. He had wood left, so he added a porch to keep out the rain and the snow.

"John William, dear," Annie said one day, "I think we need . . . a cradle."

"Oh, my dear!" he said as he hugged his wife. "I'll build it right away!"

And that's what John William did. The cradle was made from their own maple wood and was sanded smooth as silk. Annie knit tiny clothes while John William carved a design into each end of the new cradle.

"That's just what we need," Annie said when she saw the lovely work he'd done. "John William, dear," Annie said one day, "I think we need . . .

. . . some bedrooms. And a proper kitchen. After all, your sweet old parents are coming to live with us. I'll be happy to have them . . . when I have a proper kitchen."

"I'll build them," he said and tried to go back to sipping his tea and watching the sun set behind the far hills. But it was hard to do with his wife standing there, waiting, while she balanced their wee baby daughter on her hip, and the children played around him. He sighed and put down his cup. "Right away, my dear," he said.

And that's what John William did. In the loft above the one room, he built three small bedrooms. He traded wood to the brickmaker and added a chimney to the new kitchen so Annie could have one of those fancy cooking stoves. In the evenings, John William fashioned a rocking chair for each side of the stove where his sweet old parents could rest.

"That's just what we need," they said when they saw the lovely work he'd done.

"John William, dear," Annie said one day, "I think we need . . .

. . . another house added on to this one."

"But, my dear!" he cried. "Another house?"

"Well, with Aunt Rachel coming to help with the housekeeping and my cousin, Archie Neil, needing a home since he was injured in the woods, we've run out of room. And you know Mrs. MacPhee, who was widowed when the mine collapsed, has nowhere to go. She's the best spinner and weaver in the county, though, and could earn her keep, what with all the sheep you've added to the flock."

"Stop!" he said. "All right! I'll build it right away."

And that's what John William did. His son, John Hugh, was old enough to help. They built it big and they built it strong, with eight rooms and a large central hallway. The new staircase with the fancy banister had a very gentle rise so the young children and the old folks would have an easy time of it climbing to their bedrooms.

"That's just what we need," Annie said when she saw the lovely work they'd done.

"John William, dear," Annie said one day, "I think we need . . .

. . . a double parlor on the west side of the house."

"Yes, dear," her husband said, and waited.

"And, maybe, just two more bedrooms above the new parlor."

"Is that all?" he asked.

"Oh, yes, John William," Annie said. "I don't want you to work too hard."

"Good enough," he said. "And who's moving in now to sleep in these new bedrooms?"

"Don't be silly, John William, dear. We will occupy one of them, and your sweet old parents will have the other. Of course," she went on, "then we'll have plenty of room for . . .

. . . your poor widowed sister and her poor orphaned grandchild,
who've been alone – alone since the Big Flu. Flora hardly keeps body
and soul together with only her few coins from giving the music lessons."

"You're right, my dear," he said. "I'll build them right away."

And that's what John William did. It was lucky he had four grown sons
and two helpful daughters, or they'd never have been done before the
autumn storms came.

"That's just what we need," Annie said when she saw the lovely work
they'd done.

Well, by now, there were seventeen rooms. It was a good thing because,
by now, twenty people lived there.
Sons and daughters had gotten married.
Grandchildren had started arriving.
Distant relatives and close neighbors
came and went. John William had
thirty head of cattle, twenty-four
sheep, a large chicken coop, and
two barns filled with winter hay.

All the family and all the friends helped, and they had the loveliest ceilidhs in the new double parlor.

"John William, dear," Annie said one day, "I think we need —"

"Not another word," her husband said, "until I get my toolbox. All right, my dear, tell me what we need now."

"John William, dear," Annie said, "I think we need . . .

. . . to retire."

"Good enough!" he said.

And that's what they did. Their sons and sons-in-law built them a cozy cottage at the edge of the apple orchard. Their daughters and daughters-in-law painted it and made curtains. Their grandchildren brought wildflowers and fresh bread every other day. Each evening they sat by their door, sipped their tea, and watched the sun set behind the far hills. They could see the goings-on down at the main house.

"This is all we need," John William and Annie Smith said when they saw the lovely work they'd done.